Bright
≡Summaries.com

A Simple Heart

by Gustave Flaubert

BOOK ANALYSIS

Written by Sandrine Guihéneuf
Translated by Oliver Brown

A Simple Heart

by GUSTAVE FLAUBERT

GUSTAVE FLAUBERT

FRENCH WRITER

- Born in 1821 in Rouen

- Died in 1880 near Rouen

- Some of his works:

  - *Salammbô* (1862), novel

  - *L'Éducation sentimentale* (1869), novel

  - *Bouvard and Pécuchet* (1881), unfinished novel

Gustave Flaubert was born in Rouen in 1821. Passionate about writing, he discovered his literary vocation at an early age. In 1841, he left for Paris to study law, which he soon abandoned. The author then settled in Croisset, on the banks of the Seine, and frequented the literary societies of the time. He became friends with Charles Baudelaire, Ivan S. Tourgueniev, George Sand and Guy de Maupassant, for whom he was a model.

A sickly perfectionist, he defended reflective literature and dreamed of writing "a book about nothing". His work, which is also distinguished by the depth of the psychological study of the characters, heralds the many developments that the novel will undergo in the 20th century[e]. Flaubert died in 1880, leaving behind him several unfinished novels and abundant correspondence.

A SIMPLE HEART

A story steeped in mysticism

- **Genre:** Storytelling

- **Reference edition:** *Un cœur simple*, in *Trois Contes*, Paris, Le Livre de Poche, 1983, 191 p.

- **1ʳᵉ edition:** 1877

- **Themes:** devotion, affection, death, religion

Un cœur simple is a short story written by Flaubert as part of a triptych entitled *Trois contes*. This collection brings together the story under study, *La Légende de saint Julien l'Hospitalier* and *Hérodias*. It was first published in 1877, but each of the stories was first published individually in the journal *Le Moniteur universel*.

A Simple Heart tells the story of Félicité, a young uneducated peasant girl who enters the service of a middle-class widow from Pont-l'Évêque, Mᵐᵉ Aubain. She devotes herself completely to the family and is particularly attached to the two children, Paul and Virginie. The good girl has all the qualities of a good servant. Time passes and she loses all those she loves in succession. She ends her life alone in an unhealthy room, and dies on Corpus Christi; happy to find her parrot in heaven, which she equates with the Holy Spirit.

CHAPTER 1

Félicité, a fifty-year-old maid, works for Mme Aubain, a middle-class woman from Pont-l'Évêque, a widow and mother of two children. Her daily routine is routine. She is a model of cleanliness and organisation despite the lost luxury of the house.

CHAPTER 2

A look back at Félicité's past.

When her parents died, Félicité is placed as a farm girl in the Normandy countryside. One evening at a ball, she meets Théodore, who proposes to her. But in the end, in order to avoid the army, he prefers to marry a rich widow who is prepared to pay another man to replace him in military service. Betrayed, Félicité leaves the farm and goes to Pont-l'Évêque in search of a job as a maid. So, at the age of eighteen, she enters the service of the Aubain family and takes care of the children she adores: Paul and Virginie.

During a walk, an angry bull almost kills Mr.^me Aubain, his children and Félicité. Félicité prevents the tragedy with her presence of mind. Following this accident, Virginie suffers from a nervous disorder. The doctor recommends sending her to Trouville, where she feels less weak.

It is there that Félicité meets by chance her sister, Nastasie Barette, and her nephew, Victor. The young woman takes a liking to them even though they do not hesitate to take advantage of her kindness. Mme Aubain, no longer able to bear Victor's tutelage towards Paul, decides to return to Pont-l'Évêque. Paul, for his part, goes to Caen College to complete his education.

CHAPTER 3

Virginie begins her catechism in Pont-l'Évêque, accompanied by Félicité who learns the basics of the Catholic religion. She identifies with the young girl when she makes her first communion, but although she is touched by the faith, she finds it difficult to accept the dogmatic nature of the Church.

Virginie is then sent to the sisters to be educated. Félicité, deprived of the two children, now finds emotional warmth in Victor, who takes the time to visit her without ulterior motives.

The years go by and Victor joins the Navy, much to the dismay of Félicité, who never stops worrying about him. One day, she receives the sad news that he has died in Cuba of yellow fever, the news that left her devastated and sad..

A few months later,^{me} Aubain received bad news about Virginie's health. Shortly afterwards, she suffered a chest outbreak. Her mother sank into despair. Félicité gently lectures her mistress, telling her to take care of her son.

The new sub-prefect appointed to Pont-l'Évêque visits Mr.^{me} Aubain. They start to socialise and become friends. As he had lived in the islands, he had a black servant and a parrot. The bird fascinates Félicité because it comes from the Americas, reminding her of her nephew. When the sub-prefect is transferred, he leaves the animal to Mr.^{me} Aubain as a farewell.

CHAPTER 4

Mr.^{me} Aubain, who does not care about the parrot, gives it to Félicité. The maid shows a real attachment to this animal, which she nicknames Loulou, and tries to teach it a few words, such as "Hail Mary".

The bird runs away, then comes back, but Félicité, who has gone to look for it, catches a cold and an ear infection that leads to deafness. She then becomes more and more withdrawn into her inner world, hearing only the sound of the bird.

Despite all her affection, the animal ended up dying of congestion. On the advice of Mr.^{me} Aubain, Félicité had it stuffed and placed in her room. The maid's life is now punctuated only by her boss's meals and masses in church where, amazed by the stained glass windows of the Holy Spirit, cannot help but make the association with her stuffed animal.

Mme Aubain, taken by pain in the chest, dies in her turn and the house is put up for sale. As the house did not find a buyer, Félicité was able to stay there but, fearing a change of heart from Paul and his wife, who did not live in the house, she did not ask for anything to maintain it.

The more time passes, the more she believes she sees the manifestation of the Holy Spirit in the parrot.

CHAPTER 5

The roof deteriorates and Félicité, whose room is leaking, catches pneumonia. On the occasion of Corpus Christi, old and ill, after a last goodbye kiss to the stuffed parrot, she offers it to the priest to be placed on the altar near the house. The procession passes by, stops at the resting place where Loulou is enthroned and a last cloud of incense reaches Félicité's dilapidated room. On her deathbed, she sees a huge parrot take her to heaven. She dies during the procession.

CHARACTER STUDY

FELICITY

In a letter to Mlle Leroyer de Chantepie, Flaubert wrote the following about his heroine: "The first idea I had was to make her a virgin, living in the middle of the province, growing old in sorrow, and thus reaching the last states of mysticism and dreamed passion." (*Letter to Mlle Leroyer de Chantepie*, Monday 30 March 1857)

Born at the end of the 18th century, Félicité first experienced misery and abandonment: "Her father, a mason, was killed when he fell from a scaffold. Then her mother died, her sisters dispersed." (p. 30) After the death of her parents, she becomes a farmhand, then, following a heartbreak, she is desperate. Her despair is expressed in nature, and the landscape is thus linked to the character's moods.

She is devoted and loving, simple and humble in nature. There is a very little physical description of her, but she has features typical of ascetics, notably a "thin, voiceless face" (p. 5), which seems to foreshadow her conduct. As for her age, Flaubert remains rather vague: "From her fifties onwards, she marked no age." (p. 5) It is her qualities of heart that make her exceptional. The most important description given is a moral one: she is defined by her way of being. She works without interruption, is very clean and is a much-envied servant. Félicité is extremely devoted to her mistress and is obliged to be upright and exemplary.

She appears from the beginning in the shadow of her mistress. She is indeed the main character, but the first chapter explodes her portrait and her place in favour of Mr^{me} Aubain.

Characterised by great naivety, Félicité appears to the reader only through her first name, which makes her understand her reduction to the role of servant. The name itself is also significant since it refers to happiness, or even beatitude, a term that takes on its full meaning in this novel, insofar as beatitude is none other than "a perfect happiness promised to the chosen ones after their death". Through her extreme religious fervour, it is this particular state of bliss that the servant girl is trying to achieve, as the episode of her death proves. Moreover, her agony is presented by Flaubert as an appeasement, a deliverance.

A woman of great kindness, she sees all those she loves die. Thus, Félicité's entire existence is marked by sadness: "Flaubert describes a dark, monotonous character, who never smiles and whose life resembles a long road devoid of all pleasures. In contrast to this far too austere life, her death will represent the passage to a better existence. (*The Double Function of Félicité's portrait in* A Simple Heart, 1992, pp. 17-21)

She evolves more and more into a mystical figure, fulfilling her need for affection through religious fervour, without being able to step back from her faith. She leaves with a final prayer, while the whole town is in a religious procession.

MME AUBAIN

Widowed and mother of two children, Paul and Virginie, she is Félicité's mistress. "She is a bourgeois, ignorant, cynical and egotistical woman with only one set of values: money and its excesses. (*Time and Narrative in* A Simple Heart. *Introduction to a Mythical Reading,* 1993) She is "not a nice person" (p. 1). Moreover, when she died, 'few friends missed her' (p. 48).

Appearances and manners are very important to her. She does not like the familiarity of her nephew Victor, who is on a first-name basis with Paul and decides to go back to Pont-l'Evêque immediately.

Mme Aubain, wanting to make her daughter "an accomplished person" (p. 23), sends her to boarding school at the Ursulines in Honfleur. From that moment on, she appears more human because she suffers from the absence of her daughter: "The deprivation of her daughter was very painful to her. (p. 23) When Virginie dies, she becomes desperate: "Madame's despair was boundless." (p. 34) However, later on, she is even more humane towards her maid, even more tender: "The mistress opened her arms, the maid threw herself into them and they embraced." (p. 37) Thus, during difficult moments, the humanity of Mme Aubain shines through.

LOULOU

"His name was Loulou. His body was green, the tips of his wings pink, his forehead blue, and his throat golden." (p. 66) Thus begins the presentation of Loulou, the parrot whose annoyance with the animal has led Mme Aubain to give a gift to her faithful servant, Félicité.

For Félicité, the day Loulou is entrusted to her is a great day. This shows how important the animal is in Félicité's life. So she "set about instructing him; soon he was repeating: 'Charming boy! Servant, sir! Hail, Mary! (p. 66). The parrot becomes a character in his own right, a veritable divine figure whom Félicité cherishes and finally has stuffed when he died.

READING KEYS

NARRATIVE OUTLINE

Initial situation: this is the beginning of the story, the moment when the setting is set and the characters are introduced; the situation is balanced, i.e. it has no reason to change.

- Félicité is a young, uneducated peasant girl who enters the service of a middle-class widow from Pont-l'Évêque, Mme Aubain. She takes a liking to her two children, Paul and Virginie.

Disruptive element: this is an event that disrupts the initial situation and triggers the action itself.

- Virginie starts Sunday school and Félicité takes her there.

Peripherals: these are the events caused by the disturbing element and which lead to the action(s) taken by the hero to solve the problem.

- Episode of the bull; Paul's departure for Caen; Virginie's departure for the sisters; the death of Virginie and Victor; the sub-prefect gives a parrot to Mme Aubain as a farewell gift; gift of the bird by Mme Aubain to Félicité; the death of Mme Aubain; the death of the parrot

Denouement: brings the events to an end and leads to the final situation.

- Félicité has the parrot stuffed, making it sacred. The bird takes pride in a place in her room, alongside other pious images. The maid went so far as to buy a picture of a Holy Spirit in the form of a dove with outstretched wings. Loulou thus became *strictly speaking* a totemic animal: the two images of Loulou and the Holy Spirit 'became associated in her mind, the parrot being sanctified by this relationship with the Holy Spirit, who became more alive in her eyes and intelligible' (p. 46).

Final situation: this is the end of the story. The situation is again stable, like the initial situation, but it has undergone transformations.

- Félicité dies on Corpus Christi. In heaven, she finds her parrot, which she equates with the Holy Spirit.

BETWEEN STORY AND SHORT STORY

Un cœur simple is a tale that is part of a triptych, the collection entitled *Trois contes* de Flaubert, which includes, in addition to our story, *La Légende de saint Julien l'Hospitalier* and *Hérodias*. It is not by chance that the author chose to group them together under the title of "tales", and not "short stories", as was the custom at the time to designate all short stories. ᵉFlaubert, and the authors of the 19th century in general, sought to move away from this "commercial name" and thus break with four centuries of tradition.

A Simple Heart is more like a fairy tale in its supernatural ending and moral purpose, characteristics less present in the short story, which usually tells a realistic story. The final combination of reality and wonder leaves the character of Félicité ambiguous, while at the same time giving meaning to the story: it is in religion that the character has found peace and acceptance of life.

However, certain aspects of *A Simple Heart* also bring the narrative closer to the genre of the realist short story. The latter tends to represent reality in all its aspects and brings to the fore social classes previously neglected in literature. Thus, it is Félicité, a humble servant, and not Mme Aubain, her rich mistress, who is projected into the centre of the story. The story begins *in media res*, as if it were inserted into a pre-existing reality. Delegated to a trustworthy narrator whose knowledge and experience are a guarantee of seriousness, the story acquires depth and authenticity. All traces of judgement are erased in favour of an "exact uncertainty" ("The Storyteller in *A Simple Heart*", 2002). The narrative in retreat is the prerogative of the novel.

 ## GOOD TO KNOW: REALISM

Realism is a literary and artistic movement that aims to represent reality, without trying to idealise or embellish it. It developed in the second half of the 19th century, as a reaction against Romanticism, which gave great importance to imagination and sensitivity. The leader of the realist school was Honoré de Balzac (1799-1850).

TO GO FURTHER

REFERENCE EDITION

FLAUBERT G., *Un coeur simple*, in *Trois Contes*, Paris, Le Livre de Poche, 1983.

BENCHMARK STUDIES

BUENO ALONSO J., *La Double Fonction du portrait de Félicité dans* Un cœur simple, Murcia, Universidad de Murcia, Anales de Filología Francesa, volume 4, 1992.

FLAUBERT G., *Letter to Mlle Leroyer de Chantepie*, Monday 30 March 1857, in *Frontières du conte*, Paris, Éditions CNRS, 1982, p. 115.

DESPORTES M., *Les Pratiques de la réécriture dans* Trois contes *de Gustave Flaubert*, Centre Flaubert, Université de Rouen, 2003.

RABATÉ D., « Le Conteur dans *Un coeur simple* », in *Littérature*, n°127, September 2002.

TERRON BARBOSA L., *Time and Narrative in* A Simple Heart. *Introduction to a Mythical Reading*, UF, Madrid, Editorial Complutense, 1993.

Your opinion is important to us!
Leave a comment on the website of your online bookshop
and share your favourites on social networks!

Ebook EAN: 9782808686532
Paperback EAN: 9782808697934
Legal Deposit: D/2023/12603/1073

Cover: © Primento
Digital conception by Primento, the digital partner of publishers.

What should we learn from A Simple Heart, the moving short story with an almost mystical dimension? Find everything you need to know about this work in a complete and detailed analysis. You will find in this file : a complete summary ; a presentation of the main characters such as Félicité, Madame Aubain and Loulou ; and an analysis of the specificities of the work : "The narrative scheme", "The actantial scheme" and "Between tale and short story".

A reference analysis to quickly understand the meaning of the work!

PAZARLAMA KARMASI

Pazarlamanın 4 P'sinde uzmanlaşın

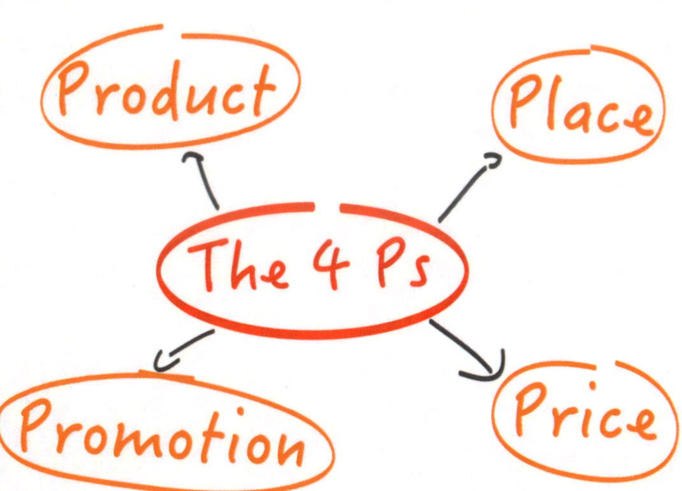

50MINUTES.com

PAZARLAMA KARMASI

Pazarlamanın 4 P'sinde uzmanlaşın

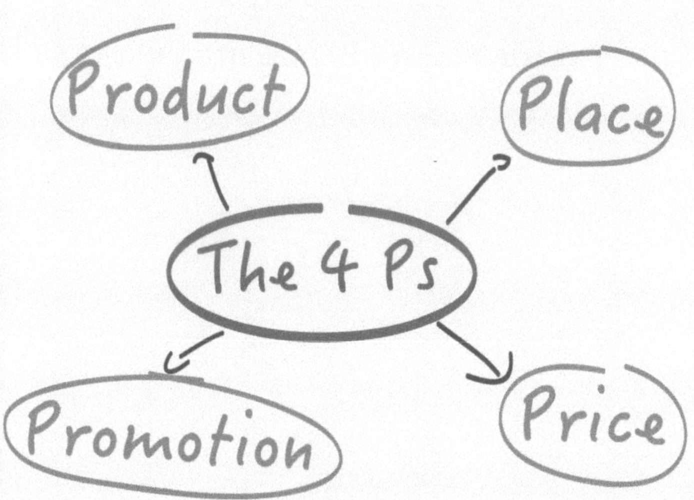

PAZARLAMA KARMASI

Pazarlamanın 4 P'sinde uzmanlaşın

tarafından yazılmıştır Morgane Kubicki
tarafından çevrildi Baris Şahin

50MINUTES.com